This Book is a short story of the Love Between

_____ _____

A word from:

To my sweet love:

Dear

"I Love You"

*1st reason
i fell in love
with you...*

I love you because
you are always

_____

_____.

2nd reason
i fell in love
with you...

I love you because
whenever am with you

_____

_____.

3rd reason
i fell in love
with you...

I love you because
you make me

_____

_____.

4th reason
i fell in love
with you...

I love you because
you make the best

_____

_____ .

5th reason
i fell in love
with you...

I love you because
you accept me with

_____

_____.

6th reason i fell in love with you...

I love you because
you understand me and

——————————————————

——————————————————.

7th reason
i fell in love
with you...

I love you because
you are nice to me and

_____

_____.

8th reason
i fell in love
with you...

Just being with you
makes me feel like

_____

_____.

9th reason
i fell in love
with you...

I love how you
encourage me to

_____

_____ .

10th reason
i fell in love
with you...

I love you because you
gave me the chance to

_____

_____ .

11th reason i fell in love with you...

I love when i spend
the night dreaming of you

_____

_____.

12th reason
i fell in love
with you...

Every time you
touch me my

_____

_____.

13th reason
i fell in love
with you...

I know i'm in love
with you because my

_____

_____.

14th reason
i fell in love
with you...

I know i'm in love
with you because my

_____

_____.

15th reason
i fell in love
with you...

I love how
i feel when you

_____

_____.

16th reason
i fell in love
with you...

I love the way you sing
to me especially when

———————————————————

——————————————————— .

17th reason
i fell in love
with you...

I love you because you
somehow always know how

_____
_____.

18th reason
i fell in love
with you...

I love the special
moments that we

——————————————————

——————————————————.

19th reason
i fell in love
with you...

My heart skips a beat
every time you

_____

_____.

20th reason
i fell in love
with you...

I love you because
in my weakness you

_____

_____.

21st reason
i fell in love
with you...

The first time i saw you my heart

_____

_____.

22nd reason
i fell in love
with you...

When i don't talk to you
it feels like the world is

_____

_____ .

23rd reason
i fell in love
with you...

No matter how bad my day is, seeing you makes all that

_____

_____.

24th reason
i fell in love
with you...

Loving you
is like

_____

_____.

25th reason
i fell in love
with you...

I love you because
you always call me

_____

_____.

26th reason i fell in love with you...

I know that you can do anything that you

_____

_____.

27th reason i fell in love with you...

Love was just a word
to me until you

_____

_____.

28th reason
i fell in love
with you...

You have this beautiful
way of making

_____

_____.

29th reason
i fell in love
with you...

I love you because
you don't think i am

_____

_____.

30th reason
i fell in love
with you...

The day i met you
my life went from

_____

_____.

31st reason
i fell in love
with you...

I love how
every time i look at you
_____
_____.

32nd reason
i fell in love
with you...

I love the way
we finish our

_____

_____ .

33rd reason
i fell in love
with you...

Having you in my life feels like

_____

_____.

34th reason i fell in love with you...

The way you care
about me makes

_____

_____ .

35th reason
i fell in love
with you...

I love waking up
in the morning next to you

_____

_____.

36th reason
i fell in love
with you...

Your smile is the most

_____

_____ .

37th reason
i fell in love
with you…

The feeling when you kiss me is

_____

_____.

38th reason
i fell in love
with you...

I love the smell of you
it seems like

_____

_____.

39th reason
i fell in love
with you...

I love you
being the reason of my

_____

_____ .

40th reason
i fell in love
with you...

You inspire me
and make me feel

_____

_____.

41st reason
i fell in love
with you...

When i am with you
i can be clumsy and foolish

————————————————————

——————————————————.

42nd reason
i fell in love
with you...

I love you because
you have taught me

_____

_____ .

43rd reason
i fell in love
with you...

I love you because out of all
the other people in this world

—————————————————————

—————————————————————.

44th reason i fell in love with you...

I love you because your
hugs, kisses, and warm embrace
_____
_____.

45th reason
i fell in love
with you...

When i find myself
feeling sad you

————————————————————————

——————————————————————— .

46th reason
i fell in love
with you...

You have shown me love
like nobody else has ever

_____

_____.

47th reason
i fell in love
with you...

You're not only my lover
you are my

_____

_____ .

48th reason
i fell in love
with you...

I love it when i'm lost
your presence always

_____

_____.

49th reason
i fell in love
with you...

I love that i can count
on you when it comes to

_____

_____.

50th reason
i fell in love
with you...

Thank you for staying
even if i was

_____

_____.

Thank You For

Purchasing This Book

May Your Love

For Each Other

Last For

Infinity

Made in the USA
Monee, IL
02 May 2022